Why(r)us the Virus

Written and Illustrated by
Kathleen Finnegan

PUTZSTEIN

Dedicated to Richie and Keira,
who have been having fun even in a pandemic because
they have a great mom, and to my great mom Anita
who has been unable to be with family because of the
virus safety measures for the elderly.

Library of Congress Control Number: 2020941669

ISBN (hardcover): 9781662902833
ISBN (paperback): 9781662902840
eISBN: 9781662902857

Seira and Sami lay on their tummies
watching an ant carry a leaf on its back.
'I miss my friends' sighed Sami.
'Then why don't you go to school?' asked Seira.
'It's the Whyrus' said Sami.
'Oh' said Seira. 'What is a Whyrus?'
'Something that keeps us from having any fun!'
grumped Sami.
'Nothing can do that!' said Seira. 'Tag! You're it!'
And off she ran. Sami chased her.
No one chased the Whyrus. Never.

Tired after tag, Sami and Seira lay down on the grass in the backyard to look for airplanes but only saw clouds.

Sami found a pterodactyl cloud.

Seira found a duckie cloud.

At last they found a large airplane.

No one found a Whyrus.

Never, not ever.

'I wish we could go to the playground,'
complained Sami, 'but we can't.'
'Why not?' asked Seira.
'It's the Whyrus' Sami stated flatly.
'Oh that again' said Seira.
'Sami, does the Whyrus stop everything?'
'No' explained Sami 'just the fun stuff.'
Seira thought being with Sami was fun but said
'I miss the playground.
I bet the playground misses us too.'
It was true. The playground did miss the children.
The playground did NOT miss the Whyrus.
Never, not ever, no way.

'But how does the Whyrus stop us?' asked Seira.

'The Whyrus is making people sick,' Sami told her patiently 'so we have to stay home and not hug or kiss people and wash our hands A LOT and sometimes wear masks until the Whyrus goes away.'

Seira liked singing Happy Birthday when she washed her hands. She liked the way the bubbles felt.

The Whyrus did NOT like soap or water or bubbles OR singing. Never, not ever, no way, no how.

'Why do we wear masks?' asked Seira. 'So the Whyrus doesn't know who we are?'

Sami shook his head.

'I wear my mask to keep my germs to myself. And your mask keeps your germs with you. That helps keep other people safe.'

'Hooray! We are SUPERHEROES!' cheered Seira.

'Hmmm...' said Sami 'maybe we ARE superheroes – we are sort of saving the world'.

'Well, THIS Superhero does not like that Whyrus' said Seira. 'I don't think anyone does' said Sami, and they ran off to their superhero playhouse.

It was true. No one liked the Whyrus.

Never, not ever, no way,

no how, no sir.

After lunch in the playhouse, Seira asked 'Can we play
hide and seek?'

'Sure!' said Sami.

Seira covered her eyes and counted, '1...2 ...3 ...' ...

Sami hid behind a big bush. Seira found him pretty
quickly. When it was Seira's turn to hide, she hid
behind the playhouse. Sami counted to 10 and then
went looking for Seira.

No one looked for the Whyrus.

Never, not ever, no way, no how, no sir, no ma'am.

Later in the day, Sami and Seira watched raindrops roll down the windows and made steamy cloud faces with their breath.

'I don't like rain.' said Sami.

'The flowers like rain' Seira reminded him.

'But the rain will wash away our chalk pictures!' said Sami 'I like my drawings.'

'Me too!' said Seira.

No one asked if the Whyrus liked the drawings.

Never, not ever, no way, no how, no sir, no ma'am, not happening now.

'We can draw them again!' said Seira.

Sami frowned. 'We can't do chalk now.'

'Oh no' said Seira. 'Is it because of the Whyrus?'

'No, not the Whyrus. It's because it's still raining!'
said Sami. No one asked if the Whyrus likes rain.

Never, not ever, no way, no how, no sir, no ma'am, not
happening now, no chance.

'Well, can the Whyrus stop us from splashing in puddles?' Seira continued.

'Nope' said Sami. 'Not if they are our own puddles in our own yard.'

'And can we have hot chocolate after?' asked Seira.

'Probably' said Sami and they ran to the closet to get their rain gear on.

No one let the Whyrus splash in the puddles.

Never, not ever, no way, no how, no sir, no ma'am, not happening now, no chance, no dice.

After they put on their boots and raincoats and splashed and chased raindrops, they came inside for hot chocolate.

'Look!' exclaimed Seira 'A rainbow! The Whyrus didn't stop the rainbow!'

Sami sipped his hot chocolate and licked melted marshmallows off his lips.

'Yep' said Sami 'Looks like the Whyrus can't stop the rain OR the rainbow.'

'Yep' said Seira 'or the hot chocolate!'

No one shared their hot chocolate with the Whyrus. Never, not ever, no way, no how, no sir, no ma'am, not happening now, no chance, no dice, nothing it can do.

When their hot chocolate was gone, so was the
rainbow, but the rain was back. Sami started to sing.
'Rain, rain go away, come again another day'
Seira made up her own song. She sang:
Whyrus, the virus,
You don't have to live with us,
Please go far away
Find another place to stay

'That's a good song' said Sami, and they sang it again, just for fun.
'Do you want to do a puzzle or build a fort?' asked Sami.
'Let's build a fort and do a puzzle inside it!' said Seira.
'Okay!' said Sami and they raced to the couch to get the cushions.

No one saved a spot in the fort for the Whyrus.
Never, not ever, no way, no how, no sir, no ma'am, not happening now, no chance, no dice, nothing it can do, uh uh.

When quiet time was over, the sun was out and the sidewalks were dry.

Sami got the chalk, and they went outside.

Seira pointed to a fluffy flower by the steps. 'Look, Sami, there's a wishing wand!' she said.

'That's an old dandelion' said Sami.

Sami sniffed the flower and part of the flower flew off and landed on his nose!

Seira giggled. 'Make a wish and blow!' said Seira.

'I wish the Whyrus would go away!' said Sami. And he blew all the fluffy off the wand.

'Yeah' said Seira. 'Me too.'

No one asked the Whyrus what it would wish for.

Never, not ever, no way, no how, no sir, no ma'am, not happening now, no chance, no dice, nothing it can do, uh uh, not once.

After dinner and baths, Seira and Sami got ready for bed.

'What a fun day' whispered Seira.

'Yes it was' said Sami.

'Did we make the Whyrus go away today?' she asked.

'I don't think so' said Sami. 'Maybe tomorrow.'

'Yeah' said Seira 'Maybe tomorrow. I love you, Sami.'

'I love you, Seira' he whispered back.

They tucked their pillow books under their pillows and went to sleep.

No one dreamed about the Whyrus.

Never, not ever, no way, no how, no sir, no ma'am, not happening now, no chance, no dice, nothing it can do, uh uh, not once, so no thank you.

 And when they woke up the sun kept shining and the birds kept singing and some days it rained but they kept having fun. Nurses and doctors kept helping sick people get well. Scientists kept working on a super medicine called a vaccine that protects us from getting sick. Farmers kept planting corn and beans and watermelon. Everyone worked very hard to make the Whyrus go away until finally one day...

...Sami and Seira's wish came true and the Whyrus went away.

No one knew exactly why the Whyrus went away. It could have been the vaccine AND the hand washing AND the masks AND not going to playgrounds AND not going to school.

There were probably a lot of reasons. Seira and Sami liked to think that the Whyrus built a rocket and left for another planet.

Maybe that's true, maybe it's not... but no one EVER missed the Whyrus.

And Sami and Seira and their friends had even more fun together every day, IF that is even possible.

They still washed their hands a lot, though because they didn't want the Whyrus to ever, ever, ever come back!

Never, not ever, no way, no how, no sir, no ma'am, not happening now, no chance, no dice, nothing it can do, uh uh, not once, so

NO THANK YOU!!!

The Whyrus Song
(to the tune of 'Rain, Rain, Go Away')

Whyrus, the virus,
You don't have to live with us.

Please go far away
Find another place to stay

'Til you do, I will ask
Everyone to wear a mask.

I'll save you. You'll save me,
Wash your hands and sing with me!
[repeat if you are washing your hands]

Why(r)us the Virus